Desmond the Dog Detective

THE CASE OF THE LONE STRANGER

Desmond
the Dog Detective

THE CASE OF THE LONE STRANGER
---

by HERBERT BEST

Illustrated by LILIAN OBLIGADO

THE VIKING PRESS · NEW YORK

For the Westwoods

Desmond the Dog Detective

THE CASE OF THE LONE STRANGER

Chapter 1

It was one of those scorching days in late summer that humans call "dog days." Desmond, being a dog, didn't think that was quite fair. After all, it was the humans who made the weather; you could hear the Radio Man every morning, telling people what kind of a day he was going to give them.

This was the kind of morning when the best place to stay was under the front porch. Once he had wriggled past the old hand mower, some garden hose, the croquet hoops, and the bean poles, there was a lovely shallow pit Desmond had dug for himself in the cool damp earth. Gus, being a boy, had a peach basket to sit on, as he wasn't supposed to touch the ground except with his hind paws.

And there they were, peaceful as peaceful, just watching the day grow hotter and hotter outside, and wondering what they would do next, if they really wanted to do anything. Desmond didn't.

Then came the frightened *Yip yip yip* from the dog across the street.

Gus jumped up. "That's Miss Petty, the Stamfords' peke," he said, as though Desmond didn't know. "And she's in trouble."

They were out from under the porch like a flash, Desmond leading, for Gus had only two legs to run on. They crossed the road and raced up the garden to the back of the house. There was Miss Petty going round and round the Stamfords' new swimming pool. A good dozen yellow-jacket wasps were trying to get their stingers into her thick fur.

Grownups were looking out of windows, but they were too far away to help. Desmond did the only thing he could think of. He shoved her into the pool, and went in after her. Perhaps with all that fur she couldn't swim.

He paddled with her to the ladder at the shallow end, but neither he nor Miss Petty could climb it. So Gus had to lean down and haul them out. You could always depend on Gus.

Then Lucille ran up. She was two years older than Gus, and, besides, she was a girl—which meant she could misunderstand as easily as a grownup. She shrieked, "Get out of here, Gus! And take your big black murdering dog out of our yard!"

Poor little Miss Petty was doing her best to explain that the day was so hot that she had started to dig a little hole in the cool ground, and had dug up a yellow-jacket nest, and Desmond had saved her life. But Lucille wouldn't listen.

Desmond knew he didn't look much like a hero. His

shining black coat was dull and matted. His beautiful white
shirt front looked like any other shirt front that has been
washed and not dried. And that fine plumed tail with the
white tip looked more like the kind of tail that rats wear.
No wonder Lucille got the wrong idea.

So he gave himself a good shake.

Lucille stepped backward so her dress wouldn't be
spotted. And as she was standing on the very edge of the
pool—well!

She was still yelling when she went under.

A lot of grownups ran to help her out. But nobody was
likely to listen to the true story. "Let's go home," said Gus
to Desmond. And they went back to under-the-porch.

And here they were again, cool as cool. Desmond was
cooler than before, because his coat was nice and damp.

"It's a funny thing," said Gus. "When we're kind to
people they don't understand. There's life guards at the
beach, and firemen." Gus went on thinking aloud. "They
save people just the way you saved Miss Petty, and people
say nice things about them in the newspapers. Sometimes
they give them medals."

Desmond shook his head to get some water out of his
left ear, and the medal on his collar clicked against his dog
tag. The medal had come in a cereal package, and it read
"Private Eye." He didn't think the Stamfords would give
him a medal for what had happened this morning.

"Maybe you've got to choose the right day," said Gus.
"Like being kind to Father on Father's Day, and being
specially nice to Mother on Mother's Day, and not getting
the days mixed up. There's a Columbus Day for people to

be kind to Columbus, though I kind of think he's dead. There's a George Washington Day too, though I know *he's* dead."

For his weight and size Gus could do more thinking than anyone in Newtown. And he was right most of the time!

"What we need is more practice," said Desmond to himself. "It stands to reason you can't do a thing right if you haven't practiced it hard."

Gus had the same idea. He said, "What we need is someone to practice on."

"And a Be Kind to Humans Day, so people will understand," thought Desmond.

Gus had the same thought. He really was a smart guy. He said, "Let's have a Be Kind to Humans Day. Then we could go out and be kind to just anybody. And folks would understand."

Desmond wasn't quite sure. Anyway, what he wanted to do most was just sit here in the cool and let Gus go on thinking.

But Gus gave a kind of a yelp and pointed. "There he is! Look, Desmond, you lazy old dog, you! There's a boy we can start practicing on."

By just turning his head Desmond could see the boy. He was walking along the sidewalk, and the top part of him showed above the fence. He wore a pair of dark glasses, and he held a book right up in front of his face. He was reading a book in the middle of the morning, in the middle of the school vacation! Gus was right; a boy like that did need someone to be kind to him. He was a stranger in town, too.

They went out and followed the boy down the street. The next thing Desmond noticed was that the boy with the book had no dog with him. Of course, there were dog-less boys in Newtown, though not many. But there would usually be a dog or two, whose own boys were busy in-doors, who would follow a dogless boy around and keep an eye on him.

The streets were empty except for a few cars crawling slowly up and down. It made you hot even to look at them. Not that the strange boy did look at them. He walked straight on, his head still in his book. He didn't so much as look up when he came to the marvelous brand-new Super-market, just opened a week ago.

The boy marched straight up to the big glass door. In just two more steps he would have bumped his nose against

it, but—the door swung open for him! He walked on in.
The door waited till the boy was safely through, then
closed behind him. And not a hand had touched that big,
shining, heavy, glass door!

Gus let out a whistle of surprise. Desmond couldn't
whistle, but he was just as astonished.

They turned in at the drugstore opposite. Being so astonished makes you thirsty, and there's nothing like an ice-
cream cone at times like that. Gus understood, and ordered
a triple-dip cone, so he would have some left over for Desmond.

A man in an old straw hat who went round cutting
people's lawns was talking to Mr. Mason across the counter.

"You heard any more about them burglars that's been
operating around here?" he asked. "The ones that cleaned
out the A and P down at River Mills last week?"

Mr. Mason rang up Gus's fifteen cents and put his coins
into the cash register. "It don't hardly concern me," he
said, "seeing I take my cash to the bank each night. And
if it's a real gang, as the paper says, they won't waste their
time on a corner drugstore."

He had hardly finished speaking when Gus said, "Look,
Desmond!" Desmond ran to the glass door, because the
window was too high for him to see through. And there
was that strange boy coming out of the Supermarket. The
big store windows showed him clearly. He tucked a paper
bag under his arm, and was opening his book again to read,
when he came face to face with the door—and walked
straight on through it! It wasn't the same door, but it
opened for him in just the same way. What a boy!

"Gosh!" said Gus.

They had a choice between following the boy and finishing the ice-cream cone. Desmond and Gus finished the ice cream, since the boy wouldn't melt. And by that time, of course, the boy had disappeared. Maybe he had come to a wall or something, and it had opened and let him through. That trick of his would be mighty handy to know, especially for a dog who was always getting his tail caught in doors.

Late that evening, when most of the dogs had seen their boys to bed, Desmond was sitting out on the porch, still thinking. He was allowed to sleep there in hot weather, after the furniture had been turned up and all the nice soft cushions had been taken indoors.

Without Gus to help him, Desmond's thinking hadn't got very far. He could see that Gus was going to be disappointed if he couldn't be kind to humans. But how was Gus going to be kind to a boy who didn't even need to open a door for himself?

Maybe Bill the boxer would know. Desmond decided that, since the evening was cooler now, he would trot round and see Bill.

Bill the boxer was as famous as he was handsome. He had won more show ribbons than any other dog in Newtown. He had his own house to sit and think in. His two boys weren't allowed to sit in it, though he could walk into theirs whenever he wanted to. His was called the Doghouse, because it was for dogs only, and very special. Desmond found him lying beside his door, enjoying the evening breeze, and ready for a chat.

With all his experience Bill could answer almost any question. But Desmond's problem about how to be kind to the Book Boy puzzled him.

Bill frowned till he looked almost like a bloodhound. "If the boy likes books, you could give him one. But not any kind of a book. From what I've heard, there's as much difference between book and book as there is between bone and bone. Now, there's bones you crack for the marrow inside; there's bones you chew on because they're crunchy; there's bones that have meat on them. It's the same with books."

All books smelled much the same to Desmond, so this was hard to believe. "You mean it's no good giving the Book Boy a book, because we wouldn't know what kind to give him?"

Bill gave a lazy grunt which meant "yes." "One dog and one boy aren't going to be enough to handle the problem. If I were you, Desmond, I'd get two or three other fellows to help."

But he crossed one elegant brown paw over the other and closed his eyes, to show *he* didn't intend to run around helping.

Still, that was good advice. So when Gus and Desmond waited for the Book Boy next morning, and went out to be kind to him, Desmond looked around for a dog or two to lend a helping paw. And by good luck the first one he saw was Gloria the German shepherd dog.

This morning Gloria was herding only three of her children, because two were being kept indoors for being naughty. She agreed to take on the Book Boy too, for she liked herding, and the bigger her herd the prouder she was.

"Keep an eye on my three," she told Desmond, "and I'll bring the boy over to this side of the road. He oughtn't to be in all that sun on a day like this." So she crossed the road and spoke to the Book Boy.

He didn't take any notice. She gave him a gentle nudge. He just went on walking, nose in book. She got right in front of him—and Gloria was a big dog. He bumped into her. He said, "Pardon me," politely, and stepped back and walked on round her. If he had had a hat on he would have raised it. He hadn't even noticed that Gloria was a dog.

Gloria came bustling back to her charges. "He hasn't got the sense of a two-year-old! All right, children. On we go."

"That shows how badly he needs somebody to look after him," Gus whispered to Desmond. "Maybe our chance will come next. We mustn't lose sight of him. He might come to the end of a road and not know how to turn around. Or he might walk into a lamp post and need someone to pick up his spectacles. We might even save his life, if somebody else doesn't do it first."

They picked up Bill the boxer to help. He grumbled, but came along. They trailed that Book Boy all over town. But nothing happened to him. He wasn't heading in any particular direction, so far as they could see. But at last he came to a house with an open door and walked right in, still reading. They waited for him to come out, so Gus could ask him where he lived, and they could lead him there. But he didn't come out.

"You don't suppose," asked Gus, "he really lives there?

And hit on that one house out of all the others by plain luck?"

Bill the boxer looked wise, as he always did when he didn't know, but Desmond wondered if it could be another bit of magic, like the way he had opened the Supermarket door.

"Know what?" said Gus when he and Desmond reached home. "There are folks who can't tell colors, and they call them color blind. The Book Boy's dog blind. He can't see dogs. We really have to help him."

When Alf the Airedale heard of Gus's Be Kind to Humans Week—for it had to be a week now, not just one day—he didn't need any persuasion to have a try. The trouble with Alf was that, though he was the best fighter in town, and good-natured enough to fight anyone, any time, for just as long as anyone wanted to fight, he wasn't really a thinking dog. It didn't seem that he could succeed where Gus, Desmond, Gloria, and even Bill the boxer had failed.

"This," said Desmond to himself, "I've got to see!" So he took Gus along.

They followed Alf out to the golf course, which was a long way in such hot weather. It wasn't likely that the Book Boy would be there. Perhaps Alf had some sense for once, and wanted to get a little practice on someone who was easy to be kind to before he tried the Book Boy.

That was exactly what happened. Alf went out onto the golf course, and, whenever a man hit a ball, Alf was there to bring it back to him. It saved the man having to walk after it in all that heat. Sometimes Alf lost the ball, and he brought balls back to the wrong golfers, because

Airedales haven't a very good sense of smell. Desmond could have done better, because one of his ancestors was a retriever. But it was Alf's idea, so it was only right to let him play it alone.

The golfers shouted at Alf. They ran after him waving their clubs. They tried to catch him, though they hadn't a chance, for Alf was an in-and-out fighter, and quick on his feet. Alf was having a lovely time teaching them this new game, which was far more exciting than the one they usually played.

It wasn't long before Gus said, "Those golfers are getting angry. They're not playing for the fun of it. I wonder why?"

Gus was right, as usual. Something had gone wrong again, just as it had at the Stamfords' swimming pool. You couldn't exactly put your paw on what it was—just some grownup stuff that didn't make sense.

So they left Alf enjoying himself, and the golfers getting hotter and hotter, and started for home. Gus said it was Desmond's turn to be kind to humans, whether he wanted or not.

They met the Book Boy heading across some lots, still reading. Gus asked him what he was reading. He said he was reading nature study, and that was why he was out here in the fields, where nature was. Gus told him he wasn't looking at nature, whatever nature was. The boy said he didn't need to, as it was all here in his book—with pictures, too, of everything from butterflies to water rats.

Desmond left them talking, for he had an idea. A picture of a rat wouldn't be half as good as a real rat. It wouldn't have the right smell, for one thing. And he knew just where he could find a rat. It wouldn't have moved, because it was dead.

He found it, and was bringing it along, when one of those serious dachshunds trotted up and said, "Good afternoon. I don't suppose you have seen a book and a boy?"

The dog was a stranger, but dachshunds were so polite that you had to be polite in return—even when you had a rat in your mouth.

" 'Long 'ere." Desmond pointed with the rat's tail.

The dachshund put her nose to the ground, which wasn't far for it to go, as her legs were so short. She seemed to have plenty of breath for talking. "Picked up his scent just the moment I stepped out of the car," said the dachshund. "Sniff! Sniff! I'd know it even in a crowded railroad depot. Sniff! You been looking after him? I've known boys easier to handle. Always has his nose in a book. Sniff! Sniff! They wouldn't let me on the bus with him, and his father couldn't drive down until today. I was worried about him. Ah, there he is! At last!"

The Book Boy dropped his book. He lost his spectacles. He yelled, "Duchess! How did you get here?" And all he seemed to care about was that here was his own dog back again. He didn't look at the rat.

As Gus said later, you never can tell. The Book Boy hadn't been in the least bit dogless. Not really. He hadn't needed anyone to be kind to him. So Gus and Desmond would have to start all over again, and find someone who did. Maybe a grownup this time. Grownups seldom had dogs to look after them.

Chapter 2

Gus's tree stood in Gus's yard, and a fine tree it was, if you liked trees or could find any use for them. Desmond didn't and couldn't. Trees were made for birds who had no other place to go. When cats became too sassy you chased them up trees, and sat down below till they promised not to call you those names again. Sometimes your boy climbed a tree, but he soon came down again because there was nothing up there. Dogs didn't climb trees, for they had more important things to do.

So when Gus took it into his head to climb his tree, which had thick branches and a good solid trunk with lots of toeholds on the way up, Desmond waited down below.

"I can see right up and down the road," Gus reported.

Desmond was thinking as hard as he could, "Don't forget it's our Be Kind to Humans Week. We ought to get busy and find someone to be kind to."

Usually Gus could catch one of Desmond's ideas in a flash, except when he had an idea of his own, and this was one of those times. "If I had a cushion I could sit here all day," Gus called down.

Desmond stared up into the branches at Gus's dangling feet. Not *all* day! Gus couldn't really mean that. He might as well be shut up in a schoolroom. "But how are we going to find our human to be kind to?" he thought as he looked at Gus. "With you sitting up there, and me watching you down here, however are we going to find him?"

Then he wished he hadn't thought that thought, for Gus said, "And what's more, it's the best place in all the world to catch sight of him. He's bound to go up or down the road, and I can see everything that passes. You never thought of that, you dumb old dog, you!"

So Gus had to have his cushion. Then he had to have a short plank to set the cushion on, and he found that in the toolshed. Then he found a clothesline to haul them up after him, because planks and cushions aren't easy to carry when you're shinning up a tree.

Desmond did his best. Time and again he tried to explain that if you wanted to find anything, even a human, you followed a trail. A trail had to have ground to lie on, and there wasn't any ground right up in the air. But it didn't do any good. Gus just sat there and sat there.

That evening Gus's father, who was almost as smart as Gus, got caught by Gus's idea. He thought it would be safer to rope the plank to the branches, or maybe nail it. Desmond nudged his arm and did his best to make him see that planks had no place up in trees. But Father only said, "Be still, Desmond. Don't fidget. You're worse than Gus."

Desmond talked it over with the other dogs. One of the oldest dogs, who had three boys and could spare a couple, remembered that he had let them build a tree house. But that was years ago. The boys had grown up and the tree house had rotted away and fallen. So that scarcely counted.

Bill the boxer said, "Just use your influence, Desmond. Point out to your Gus that he can't *do* anything up a tree. Not even catch birds, because they fly off to another tree. Nothing ever happens up there. And if Gus didn't have things happen to him he would go off his feed. Don't worry," said Bill soothingly, "it will all come right in the end."

But it didn't come right for a long time. That week end Father got out a ladder and set it against the tree. That was the real beginning. One plank led to another, and grew into a sort of platform high up among the branches. The sound of hammering and sawing brought a few dogs around, and they brought their boys. More boys brought more dogs, till there was scarcely room in Gus's yard for all of them. Those who were nearest to the trunk had to watch out for falling lumber and nails, and once a hammer.

What can't be cured must be endured. Desmond tried to make the best of it. It wasn't every dog's boy who could build a tree house, even with his father to help. So Desmond trotted round among the other dogs, making them welcome to his yard, and boasting a little.

Next week end Gus and Father hauled up Gus's little camping tent and pitched it over the platform, so they would have shelter in case rain came up. But there was scarcely a dog, and no boy at all, to help Desmond watch and admire. He couldn't imagine what had become of them all until Gloria, the big German shepherd, explained. She herded her children in through the gate, sat them down on the grass well away from where anything could fall on them, and stalked over to Desmond. It was the first time he had ever seen her hackles raised, so she must be very angry.

"You ought to be ashamed of yourself, Desmond, letting your boy get out of hand like this." Her voice wasn't as deep and kind as usual. "It's causing trouble all over town. There's scarcely a boy or girl left on the ground. They're all making their own tree houses, and dogs are getting cricks in their necks just from staring up. I had to promise my little ones to show them a real tree house before I could get them out for their morning walk. Imagine!" And she herded her small charges out of the yard again to safety.

So that was why the other boys and dogs had disappeared! If the other dogs all blamed Desmond as Gloria did, he would scarcely have a friend left in Newtown. It wasn't fair! How could Desmond have known that boys would take to nesting in trees? They never had before.

The next week end Father said it wouldn't do to leave the ladder out in all kinds of weather. So he nailed cross-pieces to the tree trunk, to make it easier to climb, and put the ladder away. He said, "I guess that does it, Gus, except for the wallpaper and the plumbing. And they're beyond the skill of a corporation lawyer."

He wiped his hands on his work pants and went inside the house to cool off. He left the tree alone after that. For it seemed that while corporation lawyers were tree-house builders by breed, they were not tree-house sitters. Desmond tried to take comfort from the thought, though it might be months or even years before Gus started being a corporation lawyer and gave up being a tree-house sitter —whatever a corporation lawyer was. It might be just as bad.

To get the crick out of his neck, and find out how things were, Desmond trotted round to see the other dogs. From the way they held their noses in the air he guessed they must all have built bigger and better tree houses. But that wasn't so. They had cricks in their necks, too. Some of the boys had given up the craze, not having corporation lawyers to help them as Gus had. Some had been tempted down to ground again by their dogs and had taken off swimming and rabbiting, and been cured. Dogs could do a heap of good to their boys if they were allowed.

Trotting homeward, Desmond felt so encouraged that he asked Alf the Airedale to wrestle. Alf was too good-natured to refuse. But they had forgotten what happens to dogs who sit around tree-gazing for days on end. They couldn't get their heads down low enough to grab anything but an ear-tip or a tail-tip, and that was no fun. So they had to give up and promise to meet again soon.

Desmond started on Gus right away. "Now the tree house is finished we've got to get on with being kind to humans. Just as we planned. But it will have to be a Be Kind to Humans *Month* now, and there isn't even much of that left!"

Gus came right down out of the tree, and Desmond licked him hard, thinking the trouble was over.

It seemed so, for Gus said, "We can't leave you down there all by yourself. And maybe have you scalped by Indians, or eaten by wolves, or something. Why don't dogs climb trees?"

Because dogs had too much sense, Desmond thought, but was too polite to say so. If Gus thought he ought to stay on the ground, and protect his dog from danger, that would be just fine. Desmond tried to think up a few more dangers to be protected from, just to be sure. Wolves and Indians were scarce around Newtown these last years.

Gus started to think. He looked at the clothesline dangling from the tree, the same line he had used to haul up the cushion in the beginning. Father had passed it round a pulley above the tree house, so he could stand on the ground and haul up planks and things for Gus to unload onto the platform up top.

If Gus thought that Desmond was going to climb that rope, or even try to, he must be out of his mind!

Gus went under the porch and brought out the old peach basket. He tied it to one end of the washing line, and tugged down on the other. Up went the peach basket.

"Now you sit in there, Desmond," said Gus, "and I'll haul you up."

Desmond took one look at that silly little basket, and a longer one at the terrible height of the tree. Then he walked off and lay down under the currant bushes. He couldn't say "No" more plainly.

Gus came scrambling after him, and chased him round and round the bushes, and even over the rose beds. They had a lovely long game of tag. It was lovely for Desmond, but Gus didn't seem to enjoy it. He stopped at last and said, "Honest, if you weren't my own old dog I'd throw things at you!" He looked really upset.

Just to please Gus, Desmond pretended he hadn't understood before, and went back and sat in the basket.

"That's better!" said Gus, and laid hold of the clothesline. He tugged and tugged. But Desmond was too heavy. All Gus could do was haul himself a foot or two off the ground, while Desmond sat in the basket and tried to hide his grin. This was a new game. This was fun. Desmond was willing to play it all day.

But Gus wasn't. He gave up and came and sat beside Desmond on the ground. He was too hot to pull the line any longer. He was almost too hot to think. Now was the chance. Desmond would think for him.

Desmond thought hard. "How about our Be Kind to Humans Month? Why don't we look for that grownup we want to find?" He thought those thoughts over and over again.

All Gus said was, "I know! We'll go ask Mr. Titus. He's an inventor. He'll invent some way we can haul a lazy old dog up into a tree house. You see if he doesn't."

So they went through the hedge into next door. Mr. Titus was working in his little workshop. He had plenty of time, now that he had stopped being head of a bank. So he came back with them, and they showed him what was needed.

He saw at once. "What you want is an electric hoist. I've got one that I don't use. We'll fix it up in the tree, run an electric lead from the outlet on the back porch, and make a kind of dog elevator. But we'll need something stronger than a basket. I think I've got a wooden crate that will do." Mr. Titus's shop was always full of things he wasn't using at the moment, and they came in handy to lend to other people.

Desmond walked off and left them to it. He trotted around town to find out how other dogs were getting on with their boys and their tree houses. Most of the dogs had been luckier than Desmond, for there were only a few left sitting under trees and waiting for their boys to come down. One boy had a chair tied in an old apple tree not ten feet from the ground. Another had a clutter of sticks tied every which way like a badly made bird's nest. He didn't look at all comfortable in it, and his dog thought he would be cured by tomorrow, especially if it rained.

Desmond headed home at a brisk trot, grinning to himself. That tree-house craze was as good as finished. In a day or two Gus would be back on the ground again, and ready to start hunting for that grownup they were going to be kind to. All the same he couldn't help feeling proud of his boy. There wasn't a boy who had built a house to compare with Gus's.

Because it was such a fine little tree house, and because Gus was such a grand little guy, Desmond wondered if he should let Gus have an extra week to enjoy it. When Desmond reached home, and saw all that Gus and Mr. Titus had done, he decided to make it two weeks, and not be selfish.

For they had fastened that electric thing up in the tree. When they stood on the ground and gave a tug to the clothesline, just once, up went the crate on a good, strong rope. They pulled the clothesline again, and the crate stopped wherever they told it to.

Gus was grinning from ear to ear. It was all he could do not to jump up and down. Desmond saw how excited he was.

Mr. Titus pulled the line, and down came the crate, landing as smoothly as a bird. He and Gus emptied the stones out of it. Gus said, "It's my turn now, isn't it, Mr. Titus?"

Mr. Titus looked pleased. He said, "All right, Gus. And this time you can pull the string and do it all yourself."

So Gus curled up in the crate, which was just big enough to hold him. He leaned out. He pulled the string. And up he sailed! They had even fixed the crate so it wouldn't spin, as the clothesline had when they hauled up planks. When the crate reached the tree house it stopped of its own accord. Gus stepped out onto the platform, pulled the string, and sent the elevator down again.

It really was an elevator. Desmond had traveled in elevators, and knew one when he saw it.

Then Gus leaned out of the tree house and called down, "Now it's your turn, Desmond. Mr. Titus is too big."

Desmond gave a grin to pretend it was just Gus's joke. Mr. Titus said, "Don't go up if you don't want to, Desmond."

Desmond didn't want to. Desmond did want to.

He didn't want to so strongly that he almost turned and ran back under the currant bushes. He wanted to so strongly that he jumped into that crate wrong way round, and had to get out and back in properly.

Mr. Titus asked, "Do you want to pull the string, Desmond?"

Desmond didn't. He could trust Gus, and he knew what it would mean to Gus to pull the string again. He closed his eyes and waited.

When he opened them again the cleats on the tree trunk seemed to be climbing down past him. But really he was going up. Now he could look over the fence. Now he could see right down the street. By putting his head out he could even see Mr. Titus down below. Mr. Titus and the ground seemed so far away that he had to shut his eyes for a second or two. He forgot to tell Gus to stop the elevator at the tree house. But it stopped itself.

And there he was. His legs shook a little, but he stepped proudly into the tent.

Down below, Mr. Titus let out a cheer. Gus hugged Desmond. "I'll bet you're the first little old dog who ever came up into a tree house," he said.

Desmond licked Gus's bare knees and waved his tail to show how pleased he was, too. Then, just to make things perfect, Gus pointed down to the street below, and said, "See him, Desmond?"

It wasn't far off, but it was a long way down. There were a few cars passing that seemed no larger than baby buggies to Desmond, because he wasn't used to looking

down from tall trees. And there was one man, or anyway
a man's hat and shoulders going along the sidewalk with
something under them.

"He's the man we're after, Desmond," said Gus. "I've
seen him day after day and he's always alone. Nobody ever
stops to talk to him. Let's hurry down and see what he
looks like up close. Maybe we can start being kind to him."

Chapter 3

Gus was in such a hurry that he scrambled down by the cleats, forgetting Desmond. Desmond had to bark, "Hey, don't leave me up here!" By the time Gus had run back and pulled the cord, and lowered Desmond in the elevator, Mother called from the porch.

She said, "I wondered where you two were, till I heard Desmond's voice. I've got an errand for you."

Mother went inside for her purse, while Gus hopped from one foot to the other to hurry her. Mother came out with some money, and counted it out nickel by nickel. She told Gus exactly what she needed from the Supermarket. Desmond gave a little woof to remind Gus that they must hurry.

But it was too late. By the time they reached the sidewalk there were a dozen people, but none of them looked like a side view of the hat and shoulders they had seen from the tree. Anyway Gus knew them all, and so did Desmond.

Gus said, "We'd better get along to the Supermarket, and have that done with." Desmond agreed. There really wasn't anything else they could do. Besides, the Supermarket was so new they had never been inside, and Desmond wanted to know more about the magic door.

Gus went straight up to it, just as the Book Boy had done, and, though he didn't have a book, it opened for him just as quickly. So the book wasn't the trick. Desmond had dropped back. He was determined to try it for himself. He waited till the door had closed behind Gus, then walked straight toward it.

The big rubber doormat sank under his feet, not more than half an inch, and he wouldn't have given it a thought if he hadn't just had that frightening ride in Gus's tree elevator. He braced himself to spring clear if it tried any more tricks. But it must have seen that he was ready for it, and didn't.

He raised his plumed tail high to show that he wasn't even a tiny bit scared, and stared hard at the glass door as though he expected it to do as it was told.

And it did, too!

When he was halfway through, he couldn't help tucking in his tail and hurrying, as he had to do with the revolving bank door that always tried to nip him when he wasn't looking. He glanced round. There, it had closed behind him. So he trotted on to find Gus.

It was a big store, the biggest Desmond had ever been in, and there were lots of people, all shoving little carriages. He ran around between them till he found Gus. Desmond wanted to tell him how smart he had been to trick that old door into opening for him. But Gus was frowning.

And no wonder. There was just everything here on the shelves, in all shapes and sizes, and all in wonderful bright colors. But there was so *much* of everything that it was hard to find what you were looking for.

Desmond tried to help. He showed Gus where the dog biscuits were, in big boxes, stacked one on another like bricks in a wall. Gus didn't want dog biscuits. He showed Gus the soap, though he didn't go very near because it was all perfumed and smelled horrid. He showed Gus the meat counter and the fish counter. If Gus wanted a can or a bottle, Desmond wouldn't be able to choose it for him, as they had no smell at all. Finally, Gus had to ask a man in a white coat.

Then Gus paid a lady who sat behind a cash register like the one in Mr. Mason's drugstore. So that was all right.

They tried to get out through the door they had come in by. But this time it took no notice of them, and stayed tight shut. Grownups are sometimes like that about opening doors to dogs. So they tried another. This one opened quite politely for them.

It looked as though you could do it every time, once you knew the trick. Desmond ran round to the first door. The mat sank again, and again the door opened. This time Desmond sat right down in the middle of it, daring it to close. It stayed open just for him alone. It was surprising. Gus ought to show it to Father, because there should be doors like this everywhere. Then nobody would say, "Oh, that dog wants out again!" or complain of scratch marks on paint.

"Well, what do you know!" Gus was out among the parked cars, staring up at a painted sign. He read it aloud. "Police notice. One hour barking here."

After that wonderful door Desmond felt he could believe anything. He was used to doors that wouldn't open, and screen doors and revolving doors that were no better than dog-traps. In the same way he was used to other signs that Gus had read off, such as "No Barking at Any Time" and "Silence Zone. Barking for Doctors Only." But this new Supermarket was certainly trying to please all its customers. Desmond let out a bark just to try. Nobody came to scold him. So it must be true, what the sign said. He must tell this to the other dogs.

Dogs weren't allowed to bark in their own yards, just as boys weren't allowed to play ball there for fear of broken windows. They had sand lots and ball parks for boys because of that. And now someone kind had thought up this barking lot for dogs.

Desmond would have gone on barking, just to be polite. But Gus said suddenly, "There he is. The Lone Stranger!"

The man wasn't at all the same shape as the hat and shoulders they had seen from the tree house. He was just an ordinary shape, like everyone else. It was a wonder Gus had been able to recognize him again. Desmond ran up to check on him. There was no smell of dog about him. So that was all right. They didn't want to make that mistake again, the one they had made with the Book Boy.

The man didn't like Desmond's sniffing at his heels. That was another good sign, because it showed he wasn't even used to having dogs around. That was all Desmond could learn at the moment. The stranger had a different smell from that of a garage hand, or plumber, or carpenter, who had a nice woody odor. He certainly wasn't a farmer, who had one of the nicest smells of all because of his animals.

"He doesn't look like a lawyer," said Gus, who knew,

because his father was a lawyer. "Or a banker, like Mr. Titus. Or that musician who's staying down the street."

All the same, the stranger had to be some kind of a man, or he wouldn't be here, would he?

Gus remembered his errand for Mother and started off homeward. You couldn't have adventures when you were on an errand; everyone knew that. The Lone Stranger walked ahead of them. He came to a corner, stopped, and looked at his watch. That puzzled Desmond all over again. He knew about watches; they told when it was time to go to bed, or to eat, or to go to school. Yet this man couldn't be going to bed in the morning; he was too old to go to school; and if he wanted to eat he could have gone into Mr. Mason's drugstore.

Gus had another idea. He went up to the man and asked, "You waiting for someone, mister?" That was smart of Gus. If the man had a friend, his friend would have the first right to be kind to him, and Gus and Desmond would have to find somebody else.

The man seemed annoyed. He said, "What's it to you? I'm busy." Though he didn't look at all busy.

"I was just thinking, mister," said Gus, "that maybe if you needed something—"

Like showing him where the bus stop was, or telling him that Mr. Mason gave the biggest ice-cream cones—that was what Gus wanted to say.

But the man didn't let him finish. "You done enough thinking today," he snarled. "Now beat it, sonny. You and your dog, both."

This was going to be a hard human to be kind to. Still,

that meant that no one else was likely to try, and Gus and Desmond could have him all to themselves. They both agreed on that.

So they finished the errand, and gave the package to Mother, and went down under the porch to sit and think out how they were going to start on the man.

Gus had no sooner sat down on the old peach basket than he had an idea. There wasn't a better place than under the porch for having one. "Know what, you old dog, you? We've got to have an angle. People always have angles. The trooper has them all the time. Though of course that's different. He's trying to catch somebody and we're not."

Desmond deepened his hole in the cool, damp earth and lay down in it. What was an angle? Gus couldn't explain. They thought and they thought, until Gus was called in for lunch. And Desmond trotted off to ask Bill the boxer.

Bill was lying in his own private doghouse, on the shady side of his humans' house. He had a bone, and he wasn't busy, but all the same he gave Desmond a scowl.

"You and your Book Boy, and being kind to humans!" he grumbled way down in his throat. "I suppose you've heard the latest?"

Desmond hadn't. He had been too busy. It seemed that since Alf the Airedale had helped those golfers by fetching their balls back to them, dogs weren't allowed to wander round the Country Club by themselves any more. They had to have their boys on a lead, and could go only where their boys went, which was no fun at all.

"But that was Alf," Desmond protested. "Not me and Gus. And you know what Alf is!"

"You started it. And you started tree houses too," said Bill impatiently. "Boys shouldn't sit in trees like lost kittens. It's against nature." And he snorted.

It was no use arguing with Bill. When he closed his eyes he seemed to be able to close his ears as well. Instead, Desmond told about the wonderful way he and Gus had made the Supermarket door open and close for them. Bill's eyes stayed open, so he went on and told about the other marvel, the place where dogs were allowed to bark for a full hour. He could see that Bill didn't quite believe him.

Bill half closed his eyes, and gave his bone another lazy crunch. "If I weren't so busy I'd go right down and check on your story," he said. "I'll tell the other dogs, because those are just what they need—doors they can open and places where they can bark. I hope for your own sake you'll be right this time."

It wasn't till Desmond was home again that he remembered about asking Bill what an angle was. He hoped Gus had found out at lunch time. But when Gus came out again, all he could suggest was that they follow the Lone Stranger and find out about him. And be ready.

The Lone Stranger didn't help. He wouldn't go near the river and fall in, so they couldn't save him from drowning. He didn't get lost, because he never seemed to go far from Main Street. He lived only a block beyond the Supermarket, and took his meals at the drugstore, which was almost next door. And of course you couldn't expect him to be held up by gangsters—not in a quiet little place like Newtown. What *could* be done to help him?

For all the trouble they took, it was Gloria the big

German shepherd who had the first chance to help the Lone Stranger. Gus and Desmond were tailing him from a distance, not wanting to be told again to "beat it," when the man came to the street crossing just as Gloria was waiting to lead her children across.

The man didn't know how strict Gloria was about crossing streets. He tried to shove past her little ones and go ahead. Gloria could not allow such a bad example to her charges. She was too big a dog to snarl. She just rumbled, and the stranger stepped back so sharply he almost tripped over the curb.

The policeman on the island raised his hand and stopped the traffic. Gloria nosed the Lone Stranger into line with her children and led them all across.

Desmond looked at Gus; Gus looked at Desmond. That wasn't anything they could do. Gloria was the only one the policeman stopped the traffic for. Other people had to wait for the lights to change.

Desmond had often noticed that when you set your mind on just one thing nothing else seems to count, not even a tree house. At first they used the tree house to watch for the man but they found it took too long for them to get down after they spotted him. So for a time they gave up the tree house altogether.

What puzzled Gus as well as Desmond was why their plan was so difficult. If anybody wanted to be kind to Desmond, all he had to do was scratch Desmond behind the shoulder blade, or go rabbiting with him. He could, though nobody seemed to have thought of it yet, give Desmond a fine juicy T-bone steak, all to himself. And Gus would have been pleased if someone gave him a new airgun. The old one had dropped from the tree house and broken.

They were in Mr. Mason's, sadly eating an ice-cream cone—just a single-dip one, because they didn't feel they had earned even a double—when whom should they see but the Lone Stranger, coming out of the Supermarket with a large package under his arm? They couldn't have told what it was, except that it was a large economy packet, too big to wrap up. It had a picture of a dog on the outside, so Desmond knew it must be dog food.

Gus read the name "Happy Hound." He sent Desmond out to make sure. Gus was right, as usual. Of course, Desmond couldn't read the name, but it was dog food all right. It smelled like a crusty bit of bread, but with an oily kind of smell that almost made him drool. Desmond waited to see where the man went. He went to the house he slept in.

Now, why on earth should a man buy dog food, and in big boxes too, when he didn't own a single dog? It was certainly a puzzle.

Desmond ran back to tell Gus. Gus said the same thing. It certainly was a puzzle. Then Gus discovered that he had forgotten about Desmond and had finished the last bit of the ice-cream cone himself. So Mr. Mason gave them another single-dip. This time Gus gave Desmond almost half. Gus was a generous guy.

They had earned that second ice cream. For Mr. Mason agreed with Gus that they were really on to something at last, and that maybe it was the angle Gus was looking for.

When Gus asked him, Mr. Mason said, "I don't think men eat dog biscuits. Except in the Army."

"Could the man have a dog without a smell?" asked Gus.

Mr. Mason looked puzzled. He said he guessed not, though some dogs smelled better than others. Come to think of it, he had heard of a breed of dog without any hair. Did that help Gus any?

It didn't, really. On the way home Gus and Desmond decided it wouldn't do any good to give the man one of Desmond's biscuits. The Lone Stranger must be very fond of them, but he had so many already. What on earth *could* they do for him?

"We've got our angle at last," Gus told Desmond. "That man wants dog biscuits. Lots of them. Only, how are we going to use that angle?"

Desmond didn't know either.

It was the state trooper who had first talked about angles, weeks and weeks ago, when they had helped him find the lost Mr. Titus. That was Desmond's First Case, and since then the trooper, who was a nice man and understood dogs, often came around in the evening to sit on the front steps and talk to Father.

Mostly they talked baseball, and something called the Yankees. The trooper had a deep lazy voice, rather like Gloria's. Maybe that was why some people called her a police dog. Desmond hadn't thought of that before.

This evening, while Gus and Desmond listened from the porch swing, the grownups decided who was going to win the pennant. Though, as they said, likely enough it wouldn't turn out the way they planned.

Then the trooper started to tell about a joint some men had robbed in a town down the road a way. Desmond pricked up one ear. That sounded really interesting. Perhaps the men had run away with the joint. It must be something big, like a couch or dining table, if it took several men to carry it. Whatever it was the men had done, the trooper wanted to find them.

"The strange thing is the way each crook keeps to his own pattern. And each gang, too," he said. "Whether it's stealing cars, or sticking up bank messengers. These guys rob stores, and nothing else. They wouldn't know how to set about burgling your house. Another thing—they shake down a joint once every two weeks, almost to the day. The last one was at Riverside, more than a week ago."

"So the next robbery should be due pretty soon," said Father. "I hope they will think Newtown is too small to bother with."

The trooper said he hoped so too. He got up, came over to give Desmond's head a scratch, and said good night to Father. Desmond and Gus saw him to the gate.

"Keep your eyes peeled, you two, for anything unusual," said the trooper. "Just anything. And let me know." He went whistling down the street.

Desmond couldn't think of anything unusual at the moment, except for the dogless man who bought dog biscuits. That wouldn't interest the trooper when he was after a gang who stole joints.

Chapter 4

Gus hadn't been in trouble for weeks and weeks—well, for three or four days, anyway. So when he asked if he could spend the night in the tree house Desmond waited anxiously, with both ears cocked. If Gus spent the night in that tree house, that meant Desmond would have to be there too. Oh, *no!*

"Why, yes, I suppose so," said Father. Desmond let his ears and tail droop. Oh, dear, oh, dear!

Mother said it would be all right if Gus fixed a rope around the platform, so he wouldn't roll off in the night. "And so long as you have Desmond to take care of you."

That did it. Desmond's slight hope of spending the night in the cool grass at the foot of the tree, or perhaps just keeping watch with both eyes closed, from the back porch, vanished into thin air.

After supper Gus got ready for the night's adventure. He put on his pajama top because he was going to bed; he put on his shorts because that was what you wore outdoors. Desmond ran out to the gate and looked hopefully up and down the street. But there wasn't a single boy in sight, and, what was more disappointing, not a single dog. It was the hour when dogs would be seeing their boys to bed, just as he was doing, so there wasn't a single one who would watch Gus pull the cord and look on with amazement while Desmond rose to the tree house in his own personal elevator.

Gus used the elevator first. Then he remembered that Desmond couldn't put the blankets and the cushions in the elevator, so he had to scramble down, and go up again to take them out. He had to climb the tree by the cleats after all. In a moment the crate came down empty and Desmond had to step in. He still didn't like elevators, not really. He tried to explain that he could just as well stay and guard the bottom of the tree, but Gus called down, "Who's a scaredy-pup? Come on up, you old dog, you!"

Desmond made it safely up to the tree house, and so they snuggled down in the blanket, even though it was a warm night. When Gus switched off his flashlight it was still not very dark inside the tent.

After a long time—well, maybe ten minutes—Gus still wasn't asleep. He turned over on his pillow and said in a small voice, "Desmond, what d'you s'pose that noise is?"

Desmond had heard it too. "It's only a branch scraping the roof of the tent," he thought. Gus sighed and snuggled deeper into the blanket.

After another long time—well, maybe fifteen minutes— Gus asked in a whisper, "What's *that* noise, Desmond?"

Pooh, *that* was just a silly old owl. Nobody was scared of birds. Desmond could hear voices back in the quiet, comfortable house, so it wasn't the grownups' bedtime yet, or anywhere near it. It was strange, though, how many odd noises there were in a tree at night, noises you'd never hear from a comfortable porch, or in open daylight. Desmond pressed a little closer to Gus.

"Hey, what you doing, you old dog, you? Want to shove me out of bed? This isn't a real bed, and it's a long way down to the ground."

Desmond didn't have to be reminded of that. And he was glad when Gus's arms came round him. If he and Gus fell out of the tree they'd fall together.

Then Gus must have gone to sleep, because his arms loosened. But a dog has to guard a boy, even in a treetop. So Desmond tried to keep one eye open at a time.

Gus gave a snort, and woke himself. "Gosh!" he said. "The tree's moving! D'you think maybe a storm is blowing up, Desmond?"

Desmond could almost imagine the tree was moving, though he couldn't feel any breeze.

"What'll we do if there's an earthquake?" asked Gus in a whisper.

Desmond knew what he would want to do—get right down to solid earth again, and just as fast as that slow elevator would carry him. Then he had an idea. That word "earthquake" had given it to him.

From far back in the days when he used to live on the ground like an ordinary dog, and not up in a tree as though he were a bird, he remembered Mother's voice saying, "Stop it, Desmond! You're shaking the whole house with your scratching."

He wriggled round into a good position where he could press one hip firmly on the platform and gave a scratch or two behind his right ear. The platform began to drum and shake in time to his scratching.

Gus sat right up. "Now the whole tree's wobbling! Oh, Desmond, let's go home before it falls."

Gus didn't abandon his own old dog. Not Gus! He shoved Desmond into the elevator and sent him down first. Desmond had scarcely scrambled out of the crate when Gus had climbed down the cleats and joined him.

Mother and Father were still on the porch, because it was cool and not as dark or as late as it had seemed in the tree house. So Gus slipped quietly in by the back door. He didn't want to answer a lot of grownup questions about an earthquake. Desmond lay down on the nice safe doormat, and closed his eyes. Thank goodness that adventure was over.

All the same, it would have been nice if they could have stayed up there till morning. Most of the Newtown dogs took an early walk before breakfast. After just one bark from the tree house, even Bill the boxer would believe what Desmond told him.

Next morning Gus reminded him, "We've got to keep our eyes skinned. The trooper asked us to."

The best place for that was in the tree house. That was just what Desmond wanted, now that it was daylight again. He trotted straight to the crate and got in. When those dogs came around, they were going to get the surprise of their lives.

But Gus said, "No, not you. It takes too long for us both to get down again. If I see anything unusual I promise to call out."

So Desmond was left to watch at the gate, in case he could see something, and to trot back to the tree in case Gus had seen anything. He nearly wore a track across the lawn as he went back and forth. It was another hot day, too. Gus tied up the tent flaps so that he could see out better, and took a book up with him. Of course Desmond couldn't read, but he chatted with the passing dogs. That was how he came to make his mistake.

He told them how nice and cool it was up where Gus was. They asked how he knew. He told them about going up in his own private elevator. He told them how far he could see from there. He told them how strange and small things looked down below, dogs seeming no bigger than cats.

He might have gone on to boast how he **and Gus had**

slept up there last night, but caught himself just in time. For they didn't believe a word of it!

They said, "If it's so nice up there, why aren't you there now?" They said, "Whoever heard of dogs up trees?" They said, "Just show us!" And they laughed, all the way down the street.

Gus kept his eyes skinned for the Lone Stranger. That stranger was easy to watch. He was the idlest man in town. He stood around at the corner for minutes at a time, glancing at his watch and doing nothing. Just before noon a big black car that Gus and Desmond had never seen before pulled up to the sidewalk. Someone inside stuck his head out and spoke to the stranger.

"They must be asking the way," Gus reported from the tree house. "Wouldn't you know they'd ask the one stranger in town! I wonder where they want to go?"

Nowhere in Newtown, it seemed. For the big black car swung off at the corner, drove around three sides of a block, and headed off back the way it had come. Gus saw it go.

"Can you beat it?" he called down. "Those guys even got to the wrong *town*. You'd surely think they'd know Newtown was Newtown, and not someplace else."

Desmond was troubled about those dogs who didn't believe what he told them. It might be bad for Gus, because boys are judged by their dogs, as everyone knows. If people stopped believing Desmond, it wouldn't be long before they stopped believing Gus, too. Something had to be done about it.

So when the next dog wandered up to the gate Desmond

asked him inside. He invited another and another, until there were six or seven puzzled dogs all sitting below the tree house, where it was cool and shady. All Desmond told them was, "Wait here till I show you something. You won't believe your own eyes!"

They said they'd sooner believe their own eyes than anything Desmond told them.

He grinned happily. He knew he could depend on Gus, once Gus knew what Desmond wanted. And that was going to be easy to show.

He said to the dogs, "Now watch me!"

He walked straight to the elevator. Maybe it was only an old crate to look at, but the dogs would soon see what it really was. He curled up inside. He barked up to Gus, "Now pull that cord thing."

Gus said, "No, Desmond, no! Visitors first," just as if the elevator were a piece of chocolate cake, and the other dogs must go first. Desmond tried to get one of the other dogs into the crate, but none of them would risk it. He could hardly blame them; after all, Gus wasn't their boy, and they didn't know how careful he was.

Desmond had another idea. There was the cord hanging down beside the elevator. If he wasn't allowed to go up in that elevator, he could make it go up without him. And that would be better than nothing. That would show those silly grinning dogs!

But just after Gus had been so dreadfully dumb he had to be smart again and guess what Desmond planned to do. Gus said, "No, Desmond, no!" and yanked that cord up out of reach.

There wasn't another thing for Desmond to do. He gave up. He saw his friends, or anyway those who used to be his friends, trot off home, still laughing. It was the most humiliating thing that had ever happened to Desmond. He went and hid in the elevator crate. It was all the thing was good for, anyway.

He didn't want anyone to see him. He didn't want anyone to talk to him. He was still thinking sad thoughts when Gus called down, "There! See that?"

Desmond didn't, and what's more he didn't care.

Gus came scrambling down the cleats. "It's the same black car," he said, all excited. He was talking even before he reached the ground. "It came in just ahead of the trooper's blue Chevy."

Nothing in that, thought Desmond.

"The black car stopped and the men talked to the Lone Stranger again. By then the trooper had parked outside the drugstore. I saw it all from the tree house. And what d'you know? One of the men from the black car sneaked across and let the air out of one of the trooper's tires!"

That was different! The trooper was a friend of theirs. Why he wanted to keep air, when there was plenty of it everywhere, Desmond had no idea. But Gus seemed to know. So they set off at a run.

They found the trooper in the drugstore, and told him. The trooper believed them at once. He had more sense than some dogs that Desmond could name. He went right out to look at his tires. He ran back again to call the barracks and have them radio another car. So before he could roll his Chevy to the filling station for more air, there was the big state police car waiting, with two other troopers inside.

Gus's trooper wrenched open the door. He said, "Come on, Gus. You may be able to recognize the black sedan. Those guys must have thought I was tailing them. They couldn't help seeing my uniform. Now we're really on their trail!"

The door closed. And there was Desmond left standing on the sidewalk, watching his boy go off in the police car.

Well, Gus had his own trooper to look after him. And, anyway, if Desmond had gone along he would never be able to brag about it. Nobody, but *nobody*, would believe him if he did.

Chapter 5

It's not till a dog suddenly finds himself boyless that he knows what it is to be lonely. At such a time Desmond could always go hunt up Alf the Airedale; now he trotted round to see him. Alf was always friendly. Being the best fighter in town, he could afford to be.

There seemed to be a kind of principle in life. The tougher you were the kinder you could afford to be. A little dog, not much bigger than a big rat, would scream threats before you got near her, and maybe spring on you if you weren't looking. But big Gloria would let her little ones pull her ears and try to ride on her back, and not a cross word came from her. A bulldog like Bertram would grin from ear to ear; and whoever heard of a Great Dane growling?

It was just as Desmond expected. Alf said, "I'm not brainy like you, Desmond, or I'd have thought up that lovely game at the golf course by myself. Why don't you and Gus think up another good game?"

And, believe it or not, he hadn't heard a word about the magic door at the Supermarket, or about that sensible sign someone had put up. So they trotted around to Bill the boxer.

Bill was sitting outside his own house. He yawned and said, "Can't you two see I'm busy?"

They couldn't see it, so they sat down and waited. After a while Bill opened one lazy eye and asked, "You still there? Why don't you two run off and wrestle and get all hot, or something?"

Desmond told him about the magic door again, and asked him to come along with them now and try it.

Bill wriggled back so that his nose was out of the sun. "You don't suppose I believe a crazy story like that, do you? Besides, I'm *busy*."

So even Bill the boxer didn't believe, and Bill was known to be the wisest dog in Newtown. He never said anything silly or did anything silly, because he spent his whole time sitting and thinking.

That left Alf and Desmond to go around and collect the other dogs. They came along, willing enough, because they wanted to prove Desmond was wrong.

He showed them the door. He opened it just the way he said he could, without so much as touching it. He came out by the other door. And two or three other dogs did just as he had done.

BARKING
1 HOUR
LIMIT
Police take notice

But did they say, "That's wonderful, Desmond"?
They did not!

"Nothing to it, Desmond," said Percy, who, being a pointer, was always rather nose-in-air. "Anybody could do it. Easiest door I've ever opened."

Desmond was so disappointed that he would have forgotten the other thing he had come to show if Duchess, the Book Boy's dachshund, hadn't remembered to ask.

And there it was. "Police Notice. One Hour Barking Here." At least it looked just as it had when Gus had spelled it out, though of course neither Desmond nor Duchess could read, not really.

Desmond gave the first bark himself, just to demonstrate. Then the others began to join in. It started out with only a handful of friends, but a bunch of dogs naturally attracts others. So the chorus that began to grow wasn't like anything Desmond had ever heard before. Never in all Newtown had so many dogs sat back on their tails and barked their very loudest.

It was wonderful! It was delicious! It was delightful!

Big dogs, little dogs, medium-sized dogs boomed and yapped and howled as word went round that here was free barking and that the police allowed it. The police had put up that sensible notice; they would be really pleased when they heard how it was being used.

The noise brought people running out of the Supermarket to their cars as though they thought someone was trying to steal them. As if anybody would dare with so many dogs around! The noise brought boys out from everywhere, and it brought along more dogs, dogs that nobody had ever seen in Newtown before. Some of the stranger dogs were good barkers too, once they loosened up and got into the swing of it.

Barking acts on dogs just as band music acts on boys, which may be the reason that grownups don't like bands and barking. The dogs began to get more and more excited. They started chasing each other around the parked cars. Two dogs got shut up in one, and were driven off, still wrestling on the back seat.

A few other wrestling matches started. Grownups don't understand about this kind of thing; they think that a lot of snapping and snarling always means death and destruction, though usually it's only an argument, and often a friendly one at that. Desmond took on everyone who challenged him, and wished that Gus were here to see him. He was having a wonderful time.

Alf bowled over two dogs at once, and then got tangled up in the legs of some grownup. The man sat down on him so hard that it left Alf out of breath. Duchess the dachshund crawled under a car—she was built low enough for that—and by catching at any passing legs she brought down more dogs than anyone else. She even managed to trip a white-coated assistant from the Supermarket who was carrying out a big box.

That was a mistake, though Desmond didn't blame her, even afterward. Whitecoat dropped the box, let out a yell, and ran to the hose that was hanging on the wall of the Supermarket. He uncoiled it and turned on the water.

He didn't wet Duchess; not a spot fell on her smooth brown coat. But he just about filled an empty car. **On** account of the heat all the cars had been left with their windows open. Whitecoat sprayed them all, and he did wet a few dogs, who found it refreshing. He soaked the customers of the Supermarket and when he saw what he had done he dropped the hose and began to shout, "Police! Police!"

That meant the "barking one hour" time was ended. Strictly speaking, nobody had barked for a whole hour, but dogs know that it's no use trying to argue with grown-ups, especially policemen. So they called it a day and wandered off homeward.

Desmond gave his shiny black coat a shake, because naturally it had become a little dusty. He raised his head to show his gleaming white shirt front. He waved his plumey black tail with its white tip. Desmond was feeling fine. And just wait till he told Gus. Gus would be so pleased.

But when he reached home there was no Gus anywhere. Not in the tree house, not under the porch, not even in the house. Of course there had been three troopers with him when he went off in that police car, so he ought to be all right. But troopers weren't the same as your own dog, who was used to looking after you. Father was on the front porch, so Desmond went up to lie down beside him. He'd be the first to get news of Gus.

Father was reading the newspaper. Desmond had just started to lick a front paw that had been trodden on, when the state police car stopped at the gate and drove on; then up the path came Gus and the trooper from down the block.

Well, Gus had done just as well as Desmond himself, only in a different way.

"I thought I'd come and say thank you for lending me your son," the trooper said to Father. "We clocked that black car at a hundred and three miles an hour, and had to radio ahead for a road block. But we caught them, all right."

Father asked if Gus and the trooper would like a Coke after such a dry and dusty chase. They said they would, and Mother brought them out, one each, with straws.

"Gus is rather young to give evidence in court." Father, who was a lawyer, knew about such things.

"He won't need to. We booked the guys for speeding, and left them phoning their attorney for bail."

Desmond wondered what an attorney was; it was the first he had heard of it. Maybe Gus would explain later.

"We'll be able to trace the call and that will tell us where the guys come from. Of course, we took movies of them as they got out of the car, and tape recordings of what they said. We'll have those checked and recognized by their home-town police. That's the way we do things nowadays"—the trooper looked at Gus—"when a good citizen keeps his eyes skinned and gives us a tip-off that we can follow."

Indoors the telephone began to ring. It kept on ringing. Down the street Desmond could hear another and another telephone ringing, and the one across the way.

Mother went indoors to answer the ring.

Father went on talking to the trooper. "You didn't discover why the men were in Newtown, did you? It's a quiet little town. Nothing much ever happens here."

"It might be anything. To case a joint they plan to rob. Or to look for a safe hideout, if they've got the criminal record we think they have." The trooper grinned at Gus. "But they won't be back again. Not with Gus and me around." And *Desmond*, thought Desmond.

Mother hurried out of the house. "Would you believe it? There's been a riot. Right here in Newtown. Down at the Supermarket. Somebody phoned me that it's even announced in the local radio news."

The trooper jumped to his feet. "That comes of Gus and me both being out of town. I'd better hurry and lend a hand to the town police."

Desmond got up too. He didn't know why, but something seemed to be warning him.

"Don't go," said Mother to the trooper. "The riot's all over. And anyway it was a dog riot. Everybody wants to know who started it."

They all looked at Desmond standing there. But Gus wasn't the kind of guy to desert a friend in need. He set down his Coke, though it was only half finished, and said, "Come on, Desmond. Let's *us* go find out."

You could depend on Gus.

Chapter 6

No grownup ever discovered what had really happened down at the Supermarket. The manager didn't care. He said the reports in the newspaper were as good as paid advertisements, or better. But boys who had been there told boys who hadn't, and boys wouldn't let their dogs out of sight for days. Perhaps they felt a little envy of all the excitement. Or perhaps they didn't want to be left out next time.

But it was hard on the dogs. No dog could trot down the street alone without his boy calling after him, "Hey! Where you going?" No dog could even chase his own cat up a tree without a boy being around to say, "Stop that!" All over Newtown cats were getting sassy, and

dogs were moping around, tails down, trying to look behind them all the time for fear either a cat or a boy was
there.

And all the dogs, including those who had said what a
fine time they'd had, and had thanked Desmond, now
started *blaming* Desmond.

That was why Gus and Desmond were back in their
old hide-out under the porch. The tree house was too
public.

The Be Kind to Humans Month must be nearly over,
and Desmond still hadn't found any way to be kind to
the Lone Stranger. But there was always Gus to practice
on. He was human, though far smarter than most. He was
so smart he could even wag his ears, in a weak, human
sort of way. He was practicing now, down here under
the porch.

Desmond caught his eye. Desmond raised one ear and
lowered the other. Gus tried to do the same. You could
see how hard he tried by the way his face twisted around
and his eyes screwed up.

Desmond made mule ears, twisting one to listen forward
and the other to listen behind. He shouldn't have done
that; he should have kept to the beginner's course.

"All right, you old dog, you! Stop showing off!" Gus
said. He would have said more, but a voice from above
their heads asked, "What mischief are you two hatching
up now?" It was Mother, and of course she had a right
to ask.

"Nothing," said Gus. "Just thinking." That showed
how smart Gus was, for nobody could object to thinking.

But you couldn't call under-the-porch a secret hiding place any longer, not when mothers came and talked to you there. So Gus scrambled out past the lawnmower and last year's beanpoles, and Desmond followed.

He trotted ahead, to show the way. When you wanted to know something, the right person to ask was Bill the boxer. Two things puzzled Desmond. The first was this "joint" that people robbed. Why did they steal it? Was it good to eat? And anyway, what did it look like? The second was, why did people say "Good old Desmond" one day, and scarcely give him a wag of the tail the next?

He didn't have to ask. Bill started first, just as soon as Gus had gone indoors to see Bill's boys.

"You ought to be ashamed, Desmond," Bill growled. "Newtown used to be a nice place before you started stirring things up." Both his eyes were open now, and he snorted up little puffs of dust from between his paws as he talked. "My own boy, who's known me ever since his eyes opened, doesn't trust me any longer. He keeps coming out to see if I'm still here." Bill sounded very cross. "And it's all your fault, Desmond."

That answered the second question, all right! Hastily, before Bill got too excited, Desmond tried him with the first one. Bill liked to show how wise he was.

"What's this joint thing that people steal? What does it look like?"

Bill calmed down at once. He stretched out a little flatter. He crossed his front paws. "Well, Desmond, that's a difficult question." He frowned to show how difficult it was. "You see there's all kinds of joints, like those in your legs and the ones they have in drainpipes. But nobody would want to steal those, I guess."

Bill laid his head on his paws and grunted and closed his eyes to think harder. Gus might come out at any moment and want to go home, but Desmond daren't even cough to remind the boxer that he was waiting.

"When you want to know what someone's likely to do, you put yourself in his place and think as he would." Bill opened one eye to make sure that Desmond was still there and listening. "But I guess I'm too honest to think like a thief. Now if you wanted to steal something, Desmond, what would it be?"

Desmond let the insult pass. "A bone, of course." Everyone stole everyone else's bones. It wasn't really stealing, it was a sport.

"No, no, Desmond!" Bill was quite sharp. "Think like a human! Humans don't want dog bones."

"A bone with a lot of meat on it, then. A pork chop. A whole leg of mutton."

"Desmond, you've hit on it!" Bill opened both eyes and actually stood up to wag his tail. "General George Washington used to have a roast joint on his table every day. My boy read about it. I had almost forgotten."

"But this joint takes a whole gang to steal it," Desmond had to point out. "It couldn't be just a leg of pork or mutton."

"Of course it wasn't! George Washington was a big man. He had to be to fight the British. His joint would be a leg of beef, at least."

Bill was a marvel. He knew everything. Desmond was

sure of that. And Bill was just as pleased with Desmond for giving him a chance to show how wise he was. They were standing there, grinning at each other, when Gus came out.

Desmond thanked Bill the boxer, and led Gus off just as fast as he could. Now if any gang came to rob a joint in Newtown he and Gus would know exactly what to look for, three or four men carrying a whole leg of beef. And they could tell the trooper right away.

It called for a treat to celebrate, maybe a triple-dip ice-cream cone. But it wasn't fair to lead Gus to Mr. Mason's, as this ought to be Desmond's treat. Now where could you find something really nice to eat—something that Gus wouldn't have to pay for?

At Alf the Airedale's, of course. The thought came like a flash, and Desmond's tail waved in the air for the first time that day.

Gus noticed that, for he said, "Now, Desmond, we've got to be careful for a while. You know what people are!"

People and dogs too! Desmond didn't need any reminding. He just trotted ahead to lead the way to Alf's. It was too hard to explain to Gus. Gus would just have to see for himself.

Because a funny thing had happened lately. Alf was suddenly rich. Alf had dog biscuits by the dozen. He gave one to any friend who came along, and even to complete strangers. Alf was the friendliest dog in town. But that didn't explain where the biscuits came from. Biscuits weren't things you hunted and caught. And Alf was easy-come easy-go, not at all the kind of dog to save and store.

Besides, they were fresh biscuits, straight out of the box, and he had bits of empty boxes lying around under the maples, just to show.

"Help yourself," said Alf, and burped. Alf was growing fat and lazy.

Desmond took the nearest biscuit and lay down to gnaw. Gus found a fresh one in a torn box. He wasn't allowed to eat Desmond's at home, as that wouldn't be fair. But with so many around, gnawed or whole, it was different.

"Say, I've been missing something!" Gus nibbled away. "Why'n't you tell me before, you old dog, you? These are *good!*"

They certainly were. But would Alf tell how he got them? He would not! He just said, "I found them," and grinned. He wouldn't say *where* or *how*. Alf said, "Eat plenty. There'll be more tomorrow, where those came from." He looked a bit sheepish, but not guilty as he would if he had borrowed them when no one was looking.

"But they do make you thirsty," said Gus, after his third biscuit. "How about going down to the drugstore?"

Alf wouldn't go. He had to guard his new riches. Desmond was willing enough. He had given Gus those lovely biscuits—well at least his friend had—so he wouldn't mind the end of an ice-cream cone in return. Fair's fair.

He was outside the drugstore waiting for Gus to open the door when he remembered. Alf hadn't asked him if he would wrestle. Not once! It certainly looked suspicious. Alf had something on his mind!

Mr. Mason was balancing the second dip on top of the cone when Gus said, "You know, Mr. Mason, it's hard to be kind to humans."

Mr. Mason put the ice-cream cone in Gus's hand. "That means you want me to be kind, and trust you for this?"

Gus managed to get a quarter out of his pocket without pulling his shorts clean off, and laid it down on the counter.

Mr. Mason pushed it back again. "It's on the house, Gus. From what the trooper tells me, Newtown likely owes you an ice-cream cone."

Gus put the quarter back in his pocket, as if burying a bone that he'd need badly some day. He explained. "No, it's trying to be good to someone who doesn't want anyone to be good to him."

"Never known it to happen. Not in a drugstore, Gus. Guess it's philosophy or something." And he went on to serve another customer.

Thinking of something can sometimes lead you straight to it, almost without your knowing. Sometimes it leads the thing to you instead, though that doesn't happen so often. Because Gus was thinking of the Lone Stranger, there the Lone Stranger was, coming out of the Supermarket, and with the usual big box under his arm.

Gus ran to the door and opened it. "Go see, Desmond! It can't be dog food *again!*"

Desmond trotted ahead of the man, and let him catch up. That was a smarter way than following him. Desmond licked his nose, which was dry, as he hadn't yet got his taste of ice cream, and snorted; and sniffed. It was the Lone Stranger all right. And the package he was carrying—Desmond recognized its scent. He could almost taste those dog biscuits in their box. For he had crunched one in his mouth only minutes ago, at Alf's.

Those were Alf's biscuits the man was carrying. Or maybe it was the man's biscuits that Alf was giving away.

Desmond wanted to get one of the biscuits and take it to Gus, so Gus could taste it and understand. But there wasn't a chance. The man went in at his front door, and Desmond cocked his ears and could hear him going upstairs.

If the man *was* giving them away, why to Alf? He wasn't the only dog in Newtown. He wasn't the wisest dog, for Bill was known to be that. He wasn't the best-looking dog, for Desmond was that himself, though only Gus knew it—Gus and Desmond. Alf wasn't the kind of dog who could charm a piece of cake out of a grownup's hand by looking starved and soulful at the same time. Alf didn't have a trick in all the world except going on wrestling so long after he was licked that other dogs gave up and let him think he had won.

Desmond shook his head to clear it after so much thinking, and his brass dog tag clicked against his Private Eye badge that Gus had found in the cereal box and given him as a reward for finding Mr. Titus, the Missing Banker. A private eye ought to be able to solve any problem. But all Desmond could do was hurry back to Gus to tell him that the Lone Stranger and Alf liked the same kind of dog biscuit.

He got back just in time. He nudged Gus's elbow, and Gus remembered and bent down and gave him the end of the cone with quite a taste of ice cream in it. Gus whispered, "Know what? You-know-who buys the same size and colored boxes we saw at You-know-who's! We're going right back to read the name and make sure."

Gus thanked Mr. Mason and they ran off. And now Desmond's lovely tail with the white tip was really waving. You scarcely had to tell Gus anything. He was the smartest little guy a dog ever owned. And fancy reading off the name on the Lone Stranger's package! Desmond would never have thought of that. He doubted if even Bill the boxer would have thought of it.

Alf was still under the maples, guarding his riches. And he looked rather worried. He had never owned anything before. His boy was away at summer camp, and usually when Alf was alone he ran around the town all day, having a good time. But now he had to stay home. Desmond was glad that neither he nor Gus was rich.

While Gus picked up bits of the biscuit box and put them together to read the name, Desmond asked Alf straight out, "Why does the Lone Stranger want to be friends with you? It isn't as though you were smart or handsome or anything."

"Guess I'm not." Alf didn't mind a bit. "But who's this Lone Stranger?"

Desmond put down the biscuit he had started to eat. Was Alf hiding something? Was this very biscuit part of a bribe for not telling what he knew about the mysterious stranger? Hush money, they called it, though these were really hush dog biscuits. Wasn't there something called "hush-puppies"? But they'd be a smaller kind of biscuit, just puppy biscuits.

Desmond got back to the point, a little sternly. "He gives you these biscuits, but you say you don't know him?"

"Nobody gives them to me. I go round every morning before it's really light, and find them."

A likely story! But Alf wouldn't steal. Nor, come to think of it, would anyone pay him to keep his mouth shut, for Alf was the kind that always said the first thing that came into his head.

Alf could see that Desmond didn't believe him. He looked at Gus, who had found some twenty pieces of the biscuit box, but some were front and some back, and some sides and some top. He had to lay them out on the ground and squat down to sort them.

Alf came a little closer to Desmond and dropped his voice. "Keep it under your hat, Des old pal, and I'll tell you everything. I was wandering down the street early one morning, sniffing the fresh scents, and minding my own business as I always do, when that big ginger tomcat came up. You know him?"

Desmond grinned. He sure did. Among cats that big ginger was like Alf among dogs. He didn't look for trouble; trouble just came to him. Desmond wished he had been there too.

"He started to call me names. Said I was just a big ugly bruiser, and worse. So I chased him. Right past the drug-store and round to the alley at the back of those apart-ments. Then he stopped and turned. So I stopped too."

Of course it was the only sensible thing to do. Desmond nodded agreement. You chased a cat just as far as he or she wanted to be chased, and no farther. Particularly if it was a mother cat. Mother cats' claws always seemed to be sharper than toms', or maybe they dig deeper. Even Alf had that much sense.

"Well you know how it is. You look around, pretending you've come for something else, and you sniff. And that's how I found the biscuits. In a trash pail. There were two packages that time, but only one since. One each morning. You won't tell anyone, Des old pal? I don't want to get called a trash-hound."

"You can't call unopened packages 'trash,'" Desmond told him. "But I won't tell anyway, or that alley would be full of dogs every morning, and you'd have no more biscuits to give away. Mind if I take this one?"

Gus had fitted the pieces of the box together at last. And what did he do now but tuck his shirt into his shorts and stuff the bits into his shirt?

He said, "Come on, Desmond. Let's go." So they went.

The light wasn't very good under the porch, but Gus got the pieces fitted together again, and Desmond laid his biscuit beside them.

"We'll call these exhibit **A** and exhibit **B**," said Gus. "But I wish I knew what crime we were detecting."

Maybe it wasn't a crime exactly, but it was certainly a sinful waste—or would have been if Alf hadn't found out. Why did a man buy dog biscuits if he didn't want them? And if he did want them, why did he drop them out his window into the trash can below?

That was what they had to detect.

Chapter 7

It was after supper, but Gus and Desmond were still thinking. It isn't easy to think when grownups are around. They expect you to do it with your head alone, not shuffling your feet or whistling, or scratching or turning on the radio.

Desmond flopped down on the front porch and gave a huge sigh. Gus, sitting on the front steps, tried to waggle his ears, and did wriggle his feet. Father looked at them, then back at his paper. Gus began to drum his heels on the step below and hum a little tune.

"All right, you two," said Mother, coming out. "There's just time for Gus to run down to the Supermarket on an errand for me. Here's the change. But don't be late getting back. It's almost bedtime."

The air was cool enough for scents to lie, and the streets were almost deserted as most people were still indoors, eating. The Supermarket was only a short walk away, and

they got there much too soon. It was Friday night, so the
place was still busy, with people coming out with huge
paper bags, and men lugging out filled cartons of groceries
to the parked cars. Desmond noticed the police had left
up the sign about "free barking." If they didn't mean it,
why did they leave it there? It wasn't fair.

A shiny black dog with a white tip on his tail was easy
to recognize. Desmond wasn't sure if the Supermarket
manager would be glad to see him inside. So he waited
outside while Gus went in alone.

It began to get dusk. Gus seemed to stay inside a long
time for just one errand. Maybe he had got lost among
all those shelves and all those people. Desmond changed
his mind, made the magic door open for him, and went
in to find Gus. By hurrying a little and keeping his tail
and his head well down he could slip past the desk without
being noticed.

Once inside, he almost wished he hadn't come. He met
different smells with every step he took—smells of people all hot and hurried, mixed smells of the things they
had in the little wagons, and every so often a tremendous
burst of smell, like the blast from a radio turned up too
loud. This place was *noisy* with smells. The worst were
the screaming perfumes of the soaps and detergents. Desmond held his breath and trotted past before they could
make him smell-deaf.

And there was Gus, with whatever he had come for
in his hand, standing and staring at the dog-biscuit boxes,
piled four deep against the wall, stacked up like a house
of building blocks, only the boxes were bigger and of all

colors and kinds. Gus seemed to be trying to make them answer him.

"Why would a man buy you when he doesn't want you? And if he does want you, why would he drop you out of the window into the trash can in the alley?"

That was only Gus's way of thinking. Humans often thought out loud, and the boxes didn't say anything in return. Desmond waited. If you simply *had* to wait in a Supermarket, this smelled better than most places, except maybe the fish and meat counters.

Finally Desmond nudged Gus to get him going again. Then . . . what was that other smell? It was so faint and so mixed up with so many others it was hard to recall where he had known it last. It seemed to come from among those dog-biscuit boxes. Yet it certainly wasn't their smell.

Desmond went closer and put his nose to a crack between the boxes. The smell seemed to come from somewhere just behind them, between the boxes and the wall. He snorted to clear his nose of other odors, and sniffed very hard. And now he knew it well, for he had taken a lot of trouble to memorize it. It was a smell of hair oil, and something to do with shaving, and maybe stale cigarettes, among other things.

Desmond gave a little whine of excitement, and ran around to look between the wall and the pile of boxes. He could just get his nose in—that was all. But the smell was clearer now. He gave a little shove and the boxes tottered, but didn't fall down; there were too many of them, piled solidly at least four deep from the wall.

Only they weren't four deep! Those nearest the wall

had been removed, leaving a hidey-hole. Desmond knew a hidey-hole when he saw one. And now the mystery of the Lone Stranger was clear. To make that secret den he had to remove the cartons of dog food from the stack. So he bought them, one by one, and took them home. And then he had to throw them away.

Under-the-porch was a hidey-hole, except from Gus's mother. The woodshed used to be till everyone discovered it. In a way the tree house was one. But it took a crazy grown up to make himself a secret den in a busy Supermarket! Of course, having hundreds of people walk by within a yard of you, without once suspecting you were there, would make it seem all the more secret. And there would be the lovely smell of dog food all around.

Desmond backed out carefully without upsetting the boxes. He pointed with his nose, he pointed with his tail straight out—which he could do because his great grandmother was a famous pointer. He whined, too.

But all Gus said was, "Sure, I know. It's the very same dog biscuit we ate at Alf's. You don't need to tell me that, you old dog, you. I can read."

There wasn't a smarter boy than Gus in all Newtown, but when he had one idea in his mind you just couldn't get another one into it. Desmond decided he'd have to tell Gus later, when Gus didn't have his own thoughts to hamper him.

So they paid at the counter and went out. And there across the street was the state trooper's car—not his own blue one but the official one with all the nice bright lights and noisy sirens and things on it.

"Oh, boy!" said Gus, stopping to admire it.

"Hello, boy," said the trooper, stepping out of it. "Murphy, you know my friend Gus, and this is my friend Desmond," he said to the other trooper in the car. "How about coming in for an ice cream, Gus? I think the state owes you one," and he laughed and shoved Gus ahead of him into the store.

Mr. Mason was all alone. He had a big road map spread out on the counter and was making marks on it with a red pencil. But he stopped to fill their orders, a Coke for the trooper and a triple dip of strawberry for Gus and Desmond. Desmond hoped that now, right after supper, Gus would find he could eat only half of his. But you could never tell with a boy, and like Desmond himself Gus had never been really filled up, not right to the brim. So all Desmond could do was sit down and wait; and hope.

Dogs don't bark when they eat and drink; they would lose too much of the flavor that way. But humans don't seem to mind. They go right on talking and eating at the same time.

The trooper asked Mr. Mason if he was planning a vacation with that map. Mr. Mason said he wasn't, and turned it around for them to see what he had marked. Gus knelt up on the high stool so he could see too, and continued to lick his ice cream. Smaller and smaller.

Mr. Mason explained. "You know that gang everybody's talking about? I've made a pencil ring around the towns they've already worked, and set down the date when they pulled off the robbery. And those dotted rings, they show the towns that are kind of waiting for them, as I figger it out. And Newtown's one of them."

"How do you reckon that?" asked the trooper. "You the master mind behind their schemes?"

"Could be," said Mr. Mason with a chuckle. "Here's a list of the towns, down the side of the map, with the population. That shows plain as plain that the gang doesn't like big cities."

The trooper nodded. "A traffic jam makes a quick get-away difficult."

"They don't like the little towns either. Because there's not enough in the store safes, or because anybody would notice a stranger."

A stranger? Desmond pricked up his ears and began to listen.

It seemed that Mr. Mason had run his pencil down that list of towns and their populations, and marked on the map the neighboring towns that were neither too big nor too little for the gang. So all the state police had to do was set a watch on each town and catch the robbers, like fish in a net.

Desmond didn't know anything about catching fish in nets. But all the same it did sound like a good idea until the trooper began to explain that Mr. Mason had marked down twenty-three towns in the state. And, what with banks and stores and big filling stations, there might be as many as ten places for the robbers to choose from in each town. And if you set a watch of five troopers on each place, and had three shifts a day, and multiplied them all together, how many troopers would that take?

Mr. Mason gave a laugh and folded up his map. "Guess I better tend my drugstore and leave you and Gus here to catch the fellows."

Gus and *Desmond*, thought Desmond.

So, like most human talk, it hadn't ended up in anything. But it still went on. Desmond gave a glance at Gus's ice-cream cone. It was vanishing fast. Gus had forgotten, and you couldn't really remind him, right here in front of everybody. So Desmond wandered over to the door to see if anything better was going on outside.

Late though it was, there was the Lone Stranger going into the Supermarket, when everyone else was coming out. Gus ought to be told. Desmond went back and nudged his elbow. He nudged it again.

Gus said, "No, Desmond, no! Don't be greedy. I haven't forgotten you."

Desmond ran back to the door. But it was closed, and, until Gus stopped listening to the trooper and Mr. Mason, all Desmond could do was watch. He expected any moment to see the Lone Stranger come out again, and then it would be too late.

The man didn't come out. He was taking an awful long time in there. Now the white-coated assistants were beginning to close the Supermarket, and two or three lights in the back of the store were turned off. That showed how late it was. Maybe the Lone Stranger was waiting for the Whitecoats to turn their backs so he could take out another carton.

At last Gus got down and held out the end of the ice-cream cone. Desmond gobbled it in one gulp, almost without tasting. He got Gus to the door. Gus had to go back because he had left his package. He got Gus to the door again.

When Gus was outside the door, he saw how late it was. He said, "You're right, Desmond. Gee, we'll have to hurry. But Mother won't mind when I tell her we were with the trooper."

Desmond pointed, with his head and tail, across the road, and whined for Gus to follow.

Gus said, "I don't know what's got into you, you crazy old dog. And anyway, the Supermarket's closed."

It wasn't closed. The magic door opened when Desmond ran up to it, though someone was coming to fasten it from the inside. But he couldn't bolt it till it closed again, so Gus got in too.

At last Gus understood. The Lone Stranger was inside. They ran up and down every empty aisle looking for him, while a Whitecoat shouted at them.

At last Gus gave up. "Desmond, You-know-who isn't here. And I don't know what you want to do if we do find him."

Gus was right. You couldn't just ask, "Why do you want to make a hidey-hole in a supermarket?" Not unless you were a trooper, and then you could ask anybody anything, as long as you were polite.

Then Desmond had his idea, or maybe his nose got a stronger whiff. And he wondered why he hadn't thought of it before. The man wasn't going to go home with more dog biscuits. No, he was going to sit in that little hidey-hole, and eat his way right through the whole pile of them,

and not have to pay on his way out in the morning. And *that* would be cheating the store!

It was Stealing!

Desmond was right. He dodged a Whitecoat who was waving a broom at him, and ran right around to the big pile of boxes with the dog biscuits in them. And there was the Lone Stranger's rich body scent, plain as plain. He gave a sharp bark for Gus to come help him.

He got his nose behind the pile of boxes. He wedged his head in. He got his whole body in.

And there was the Lone Stranger, crouched down, and looking at his watch, as usual.

What happened seemed like an explosion. It threw the boxes in all directions, and the man with them. But the man wasn't hurt, for he headed toward one of the back doors of the store. Gus was after him. The man hammered at the door with his fists. It was already locked. He ran back to the front of the store. And now Gus and the Whitecoats too were after him. And the manager was throwing cans of beans after him, to try to stop him.

Desmond was first to reach the magic door. That was a real mistake, for that silly door opened and let the man out past him, with Desmond, Gus, the manager—still throwing a last can—and the Whitecoats racing after him.

Chapter 8

"Hiding, he was." The manager of the Supermarket gave up the chase and turned back. "Hiding, so he could open up for the rest of his gang during the night. So they could rob the joint."

The Whitecoats turned back too. They had to close the store and get home to their suppers. That left only Gus and Desmond to follow the Lone Stranger. The man looked back and, seeing only a boy and a dog on his heels, dropped to a walk. He straightened his coat and hat and tried to look as though he were only out for a stroll after supper.

"What are we going to do?" asked Gus. "It's past time for bed, but we can't let him get away."

And it certainly was getting late. The street lights were

on and there were lights in houses, and most of the other boys were going to bed.

This was first dog-walk time, when dogs have their last food for the day and wander out to their gates to see what's going on. Duchess the dachshund asked Desmond, "Where you going?"

"We're tailing that man," said Desmond. "He tried to rob a joint."

"What's a joint?" asked Duchess, pricking up her ears.

"Bill the boxer says it's a leg of beef," Desmond told her.

"If Bill says so, it's so." Duchess stopped to pass on the news to the dog next door. "Hi, Sally! There's a man stole a whole leg of beef!"

"He didn't steal it!" barked Desmond. "He only tried to." But nobody listened, not even Gus.

The Lone Stranger stopped under a light and looked at his watch. Desmond and Gus had to stop too. They couldn't just go up to the man and say, "In the name of the law we arrest you!" They'd have to wait for the trooper or another grownup. But the grownups were all indoors, and likely enough the trooper was still back there in the drugstore, if he wasn't already miles and miles away on duty in the police car.

The Lone Stranger seemed to be expecting to meet someone. It could be that big black car he had talked to before. Only Gus and his trooper had caught that, and it wouldn't be coming back. Though of course the man didn't know that. So he turned down a side street and Gus and Desmond followed him there.

Then, behind, Desmond heard Duchess's voice, "He's

stolen a joint, dogs. A whole leg of beef. We're going to see where he buries it."

Gloria was off duty now, so she came along. Then they passed Bill the boxer's house. Bill didn't usually bother with much beside his own affairs, but it was a cool evening and he had slept most of the day, so he came too.

As he was a wise dog he saw at once that the man didn't have a joint with him, because joints were too big to fit into a pocket. Maybe the man had already buried it.

"He's buried his joint," said Bill the boxer as they passed another dog's gate. "If we follow long enough we'll see where he buried it."

So the other dogs joined in. "Likely he'll lead us right to it," said one of them. "Likely he will," said another. There was quite a procession of dogs by now, following the Lone Stranger.

The man looked back and saw them. He began to walk faster. It isn't everyone who is accustomed to taking a boy and maybe a dozen dogs for a walk after supper.

"He'd run if he could," said Gus, "but he's got nowhere to run to, now that we've found his hiding place."

Desmond could see that. The man looked somewhat like a dog on a leash, as though he were pulling to get away. He was stepping faster because he couldn't help it, but taking shorter steps because the leash seemed to pull him back.

Around the block and another turn, and back onto Main Street again. The Lone Stranger looked at his watch once more, and then up and down the street. But there was no big black car in sight. Desmond could have told him there wasn't going to be one.

And now more and more dogs had come out to join the procession. It looked as though every dog in Newtown were on the trail, but each of them kept well behind and tried to pretend he wasn't there, because no one will lead you to his bone if he thinks you're looking. The story, passed along, had grown bigger and bigger. It wasn't just one joint the man had stolen; it was a whole lot of them, enough maybe for all the dogs in Newtown.

Since Alf the Airedale had come into such mysterious riches, dogs would believe almost anything. And by the way, where *was* Alf?

"Hi, Des old pal!" said Alf, trotting up at just that moment. "This is the first time in days I've dared stop guarding my biscuits. But who'd look at a biscuit if he's going to eat a whole—big—fresh—raw joint? Maybe mutton. Think the feller'll dig it all up for himself? Or do we help him?"

Desmond didn't have time to answer. He was too busy worrying. The man had turned a corner and gone around the block again. And this was the second time he and Gus had passed the home gate. How long would it be before Mother called out to them, or Father saw them go past? And then what would happen about the Lone Stranger?

A few cars passed and had to slow down and honk their horns. But there was no sign of the trooper and his car. Boys and their fathers began to come out to their front doors or porches and whistle and call. They called and called, and then boys began to run to join their dogs.

Now it wasn't just a dog procession. It was a dogs-and-their-boys procession.

A boy said, "It's another dog riot, like the one at the Supermarket. Only it hasn't got really started yet. Let's go see."

The Lone Stranger was back on Main Street again. He glanced around. This time it wasn't just that small pack of dogs he'd seen first. It was the boys and all their dogs, and grownups coming out of every gate.

The Lone Stranger gave a strangled yell and broke into a run. So did Bill and Gloria and Duchess and Alf and all the other dogs and their boys. And when dogs run they have to bark. And when boys run they have to yell. It sounded as though the Supermarket riot had started again.

Porch lights, garage lights, headlights of parked cars went on all up and down Main Street. Cars from one way pulled to the side, so the hunt could pass; cars from the other way came hooting behind, adding to the clamor. It was most exciting!

But where, for goodness' sake, was the trooper?

Well, the reason those cars had pulled to one side was to make way for the police. The trooper's siren was going full blast, but in all the noise Desmond could hardly hear it.

The Lone Stranger did. He ducked into a yard—Gus's own yard, because that was the nearest! Gus and the pack poured in after him. Dogs wriggled under hedges, dogs leaped fences, and they even poured into Mr. Titus's yard next door.

The Lone Stranger gave one look at all those open jaws, those barking dogs, and did what any cat in its senses would have done much sooner. He made for a tree.

He began to climb it. That was easy, since it had cleats fastened to the trunk. And the dogs did as dogs always do when they've treed something. They jumped up at the tree trunk, then sat back and lolled their tongues and looked expectant. So this was where he'd buried his joint! It was peculiar; whoever heard of burying stolen meat up in trees?

Gus looked up. The man had dodged into the tree house. Gus made as if to follow him.

Desmond couldn't let that happen. He got in Gus's way, pretending it was an accident. He tried to tell Gus that a thing chased up a tree was like a thing with its back to a wall. It was dangerous.

"But we've got to get him, Desmond," said Gus. "Mother will be calling me in, any minute." And this time Gus made for the crate-elevator.

Desmond scrambled in first, and there wasn't room for both of them. He reached out and caught the cord with his teeth, and pulled hard, just as he had seen Gus do.

Gus had to let go of Desmond's tail, and up Desmond went. Quick, quick! Lights followed him up all the way. Boys' flashlights and the trooper's spotlight were on him at once. The elevator stopped at the wooden platform of the tent. The tent flaps were up, and there was the Lone Stranger, huddled in a corner.

Desmond remembered to raise his head so that the stranger would see his Private Eye badge and know he didn't intend to hurt him. He raised his hackles and gave a low growl, just to encourage himself. Then he marched forward.

Maybe the man wasn't used to seeing dogs in tree houses, or else he had something terrible on his conscience. He gave a howl, like Desmond's but screechier, and scrambled out again and went down that tree trunk faster than any cat.

Desmond got back into the elevator, since there was

nothing more to do up there. He couldn't find the cord to pull, but Gus must have remembered and pulled it. And, though it was night and Desmond hated to look down even in the daytime, he peered out. What was down below there was unlike anything he had ever seen before.

Of course it was only the tops of cars, and the tops of people and dogs, but it looked as though every dog and every human in Newtown were here, in Gus's yard and clear out into Main Street.

But, best of all, there was the trooper, standing beside Gus, and Gus still holding Mother's package. Just as soon as the elevator touched ground Desmond bounded out.

The Lone Stranger was clinging to the lowest cleats on the tree scared either to go up again or come right down. The trooper had to reach out and unhook him.

"It's a pinch! Okay, okay, I ain't goin' to give no trouble," the Lone Stranger jabbered. "Get me out of this crazy burg and keep them dogs away from me. That's all I ask."

He seemed to be talking to Desmond rather than to the trooper, who was patting the man's pockets to see what was in them. Though surely the trooper wouldn't have been fooled by that story about the man's stealing those joints.

Once the man started talking he didn't seem able to stop. "I warned Guts Gesner and Pistol Pete, just as soon as the dogs started tailing me. They claimed I'd lost my nerve. Wish they'd been through what I've been through tonight. I've heard of police dogs, sarge," he said to the trooper, "but never of dog detectives. And a private-eye badge don't give a dog the right to make an arrest."

He stopped when he saw that a reporter was holding up the microphone of a tape recorder. So the reporter turned to Gus. "Just a few words, sonny, for the Newtown *Gazette*. Same as you did last time."

And when Gus had finished, "Now it's your turn, Desmond," said the reporter. "Just a few words, like last time too."

Desmond stepped up to the mike. He showed his white shirt front, and waved his tail to everybody, and started to tell about Be Kind to Humans Week, and how it hadn't turned out just the way he and Gus had planned. That was the fault of the Lone Stranger, who hadn't let them be good to him. If Desmond let them think that the riot at the Supermarket had all been part of the plan to catch the stranger, he didn't exactly say it.

But he had scarcely begun his speech when the reporter thanked him and put away the tape recorder.

There was a lot more that Desmond wanted to say, but it didn't matter. Almost every dog in town had seen him go up to the tree house in his own private elevator, and they'd have to believe their own eyes. He would have liked to thank the dogs of Newtown for their help in catching a well-known criminal. But the Newtown *Gazette* would print the whole story, and their own boys would tell them how smart they had been. So that was all right, too.

Desmond and Gus had to pose while flash bulbs flashed

and cameras clicked, and there, in Gus's hand, was still the brown paper bag Mother had sent him to get at the Supermarket.

Everything was just fine and dandy!